Favourite Tales

DEAN

Favourite Tales

DEAN

This book belongs to

....

EGMONT

We bring stories to life

First published in Great Britain in 2008
Published in Great Britain in 2008 by Dean,
an imprint of Egmont UK Limited,
239 Kensington High Street, London W8 6SA

Thomas the Tank Engine & Friends™

CREATED BY BRITT ALLCROFT

Based on the Railway Series by the Reverend W Awdry
© 2008 Gullane (Thomas) LLC. A HIT Entertainment company.
Thomas the Tank Engine & Friends and Thomas & Friends are trademarks of Gullane (Thomas) Limited.
Thomas the Tank Engine & Friends and Design is Reg. U.S. Pat. & Tm. Off.

HiT entertainment

Printed and bound in Singapore
ISBN 978 0 6035 6338 6
1 3 5 7 9 10 8 6 4 2

Contents

Thomas Rescues the Diesels

Based on **The Railway Series**
by the Rev. W. Awdry

It was a busy time on the Island of Sodor.
The Fat Controller asked Thomas to
help Mavis finish an important job at
the Quarry.

"I wonder why they sent you," Diesel said
to Thomas. "Everyone knows that diesels
are better workers," he added.

Thomas thought he was very rude.

Diesel played tricks on Thomas. He pushed
him under a hopper so he got covered
in dust. Thomas was shocked.

For the rest of the day, Diesel said rude
things about steam engines and called
Thomas a silly steamie.

Thomas wished he could show Diesel
that steam engines are just as good
as diesels.

The next day, Salty brought new fuel
for the diesels. Mavis and Diesel were
very excited.

"No new fuel for you, Thomas," said
Diesel, nastily. "You just get dirty old coal!"

Thomas wished Diesel would stop being so mean to him.

Diesel started bragging as soon as he had been re-fuelled.

"I'm the fastest engine in the world!" he shouted.

Thomas tried to ignore him. But suddenly, Diesel went quiet.

"Oh!" he cried out a second later.
"I feel strange. Something's wrong!"

Black smoke poured from Diesel and
Mavis' engines.

"I feel sick!" wheezed Mavis.

"So do I!" groaned Diesel.

The Quarry Master came to see what was wrong with the diesels.

"It must be the new fuel," he said. "Some water must have leaked into the tanks!"

The diesels had all filled up with the new fuel and now they were all breaking down. Even Salty, who had brought the fuel, had been re-fuelled with it.

"Oh, dear!" he said. "We need help!"

The Quarry Manager told Thomas
to collect fresh fuel from the depot.
"Right away, Sir!" said Thomas,
and he quickly steamed away.

Thomas raced to the depot.

"I need all the clean fuel you've got.
This is an emergency!" he said, urgently.

Workmen quickly loaded up fuel barrels
on a wagon. It was heavy, so Thomas
knew he would have to work hard
to push it along the tracks.

Thomas puffed around the Island,
taking fresh fuel to all the diesels.

Bert and 'Arry were pleased to see him. They felt better as soon as they had been given the clean diesel.

"Good work, Thomas," they said, happily.

Thomas set off again to deliver the fuel to the rest of the diesels.

Everyone cheered when Thomas
arrived at the Quarry. Clean fuel
was soon given to all the diesels.

"That's better," sighed Diesel.

"Thank you, Thomas," said Mavis.

Diesel helped Mavis and Thomas finish the important job on time.

The Fat Controller was delighted. "Thomas, you have rescued the diesels!" he said. "You are a Really Useful Engine."

Thomas smiled happily and even Diesel agreed that a steamie had saved the day!

James and the Queen of Sodor

Based on *The Railway Series*
by the Rev. W. Awdry

James thought he was the most important engine on the Island of Sodor. He was very proud of his shiny red paintwork, which he kept clean and smart so he was always ready to do important jobs for The Fat Controller.

One day, Percy joined James and Gordon at the washdown. He had been working at the Quarry, so he was very dirty.

"My whistle's all clogged up," he said. He blew hard to clear it, and accidentally covered Gordon in mud!

"Don't get me dirty, too," said James.
"I've got to stay nice and clean because
I'm going to collect the mayor!"

Soon James had picked up the mayor
and was puffing proudly across the
Island. When he passed Gordon,
he whistled loudly to show off.
Gordon was not amused. He decided
he had to teach James a lesson.

That afternoon, The Fat Controller
needed an engine to take the Queen
of Sodor to the scrap yard.

"She is a leaky old barge, so it's a very
dirty job!" he said.

Just then, James arrived at the shed.
Gordon knew he hated getting dirty,
so he decided to trick him.

"That's a *very* important job," he said.
"An important job?" said James quickly.
"I will do that!"

James felt very proud when he heard he would be collecting the Queen of Sodor. He thought the other engines must be very jealous. His paintwork was shiny and clean, and he could hardly wait to meet the Queen.

Before long, James arrived at the canal. "I'm here to collect the Queen of Sodor," he announced, proudly.

The manager pointed to a dirty old barge. "There she is," he said.

"Oh, no! The Queen's a slimy old barge!" James said in horror.

James realised Gordon had tricked
him into doing the dirty job.

"He wants me to get all mucky!" he said.

James was more determined than
ever that he would deliver the barge
without getting dirty.

James set off with the Queen of Sodor.
He pushed her carefully along the
track, so he didn't get covered in slime.
James managed to get nearly halfway
across the Island without getting dirty.
He felt very pleased with himself.
But he didn't realise that a faulty pipe
was pouring oil on to the track ahead!

"Watch out!" called his Driver, as he applied the brakes.

Luckily, James managed to stop just
in time. Oil slopped over the barge,
but James stayed clean. Workmen
came and fixed the pipe and James
carried on his journey.

James was very relieved to leave the
dirty barge at the scrap yard.
When he arrived back at the engine
shed, the engines were surprised to see
him still looking clean.

"How did you stay so clean?" asked
Thomas in surprise.
"I *have* to stay clean," replied James,
"so I'm always ready to do important jobs."

Just then, Percy returned from working
at the Quarry.

"My whistle is clogged again," he said.
He blew hard to clear it, and this time
he covered James in dust!

"No!" cried James, but it was too late. He had managed to stay clean all day and now he was filthy!

James sighed loudly.

"I hope there aren't any important jobs to do," teased Thomas. "You would definitely need a washdown first, James."

The engines all peeped cheerfully and
even James smiled in the end!

Thomas and Lady Hatt's Birthday Party

Based on *The Railway Series*
by the Rev. W. Awdry

Bertie dropped some passengers off at the station.

"Have you noticed something strange today?" he asked Thomas and Percy.

"What sort of something?" asked Thomas.

"The Fat Controller is acting rather strangely," replied Bertie.

"I saw him staring at the sky earlier," said Percy.

"I did wonder what he was thinking about."

The reason was simple. It was Lady Hatt's birthday and Sir Topham Hatt, The Fat Controller, was thinking about his new suit that he was going to wear to Lady Hatt's party that afternoon.

"Your new suit will be perfect for my party," said Lady Hatt to her husband, The Fat Controller.

"Thank you! I'll wear my finest hat, too," said The Fat Controller.
"After all, your birthday is a very special occasion!"

"Don't be late, will you?" said Lady Hatt. "My party starts at three o'clock!"

"I'm working at another station today," replied The Fat Controller. "But don't worry, I'll do my very best to be right on time."

Thomas was working very hard on his branch line. He was moving heavy trucks loaded with rocks.

His Fireman was busy, too. He was shovelling coal into the furnace to help Thomas work quickly.

"Phew!" said Thomas' Fireman, wiping his hand across his hot face. "This is very hard work on this hot day!"

Thomas agreed. It was hard work,
but it made him feel like a Really
Useful Engine!

The Fat Controller was working at another station that day.
At two o'clock, he changed into his new yellow waistcoat and black suit, so he was ready for Lady Hatt's birthday party.

"You look fine, Sir!" said the Station Master. "But you'd best be going now," he added, looking at his watch.

"Indeed!" said The Fat Controller. "As the engines are busy working, I'll drive my car to the party."

The Fat Controller set off in the car to his station. He had only driven a little way down the road when he realised his car had a flat tyre.

"Bother!" he said crossly, as he looked at the damaged wheel. "If I change the tyre myself, I will get my new suit dirty and that will never do!"

He was just wondering what he could
do instead, when Caroline the Car
drove up.

"Hello, Caroline," said The Fat Controller. "My car has a flat tyre. Could you please give me a lift to my wife's birthday party?"

"Of course," said Caroline. "I would be happy to take you to Lady Hatt's party."

The Fat Controller asked Caroline to drive rather quickly. He was worried that he would arrive late for the party.

Poor Caroline began to feel unwell. Before long, with steam pouring from her bonnet, she came to a sudden stop.

"Bother! Bother!" said The Fat Controller, "What am I going to do now?"

Just then, The Fat Controller heard
a whistle. He turned round and saw
George the Steamroller rolling down
the road towards him.

"Can I help you, Sir?" asked George's
Driver.

"Can you take me to my wife's
birthday party, please?" asked
The Fat Controller.

"Well, we can take you to Thomas," said George's Driver. "We saw him working further along the line. I'm sure Thomas will be able to take you straight to your station!"

"But, what about me?" wailed Caroline the Car, who was still feeling a little poorly.

"Don't worry, Caroline," said The Fat Controller.

"When I get back to the station, I'll send someone to help you and repair my car, too. You wait right there, Caroline!" he added.

"That's all I can do!" coughed Caroline, as she watched The Fat Controller climb aboard the steamroller. George then rolled away, taking The Fat Controller to Thomas.

Oh, dear! The Fat Controller's new suit and hat were being splashed with George's dirty engine oil!

But worse was to come. Just as George reached Thomas, his brakes failed and he lost control!

He rolled right across the road and fell into a muddy ditch. The Fat Controller was sent flying through the air and landed up to his waist in the mud!

"Bother! Bother! BOTHER!" cried
The Fat Controller, crossly.
Thomas and his Driver were shocked to
see The Fat Controller covered in mud.

"Can we help you, Sir?" asked Thomas' Driver.

"Yes, please!" replied The Fat Controller, as he climbed out of the ditch.

"Can you take me back to the station as fast as possible? I don't want to be late for my wife's birthday party, which starts at three o'clock."

"I'm afraid our Fireman is not feeling well," said Thomas' Driver. "He has been working very hard in this hot weather and now he needs a rest. We can't move unless someone does his job."

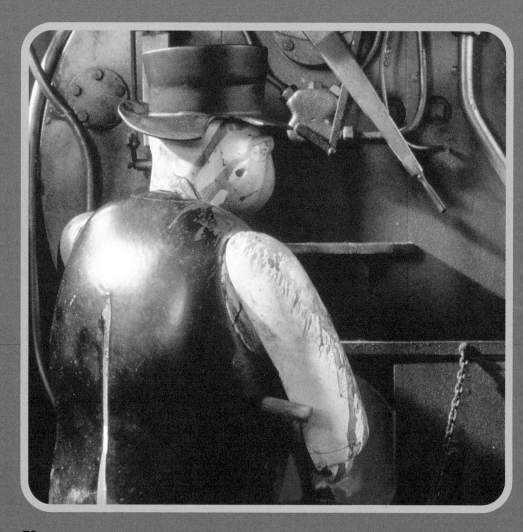

"It's not a problem, I'll do it!" said The Fat Controller.

Thomas was very proud to have such a special Fireman. The Fat Controller got rather hot and dirty keeping Thomas' furnace stoked with coal.

He was covered in coal dust too, but he didn't mind at all because he knew Thomas would get him to the station as fast as he could.

Thomas reached the station just after three o'clock.

"Thank you!" said The Fat Controller to Thomas, his Driver and his tired Fireman. "You have all done a hard day's work. You can finish now and go and have a good rest!"

The Fat Controller looked up at the
Station clock. Seeing he was a little late,
he rushed over to the flower stall and
bought a large bunch of flowers for
Lady Hatt.

The Fat Controller, in his now dirty and
damaged new suit, rushed through the
station with the flowers.

When he reached the party, no one could see him, they could only see the large bunch of flowers he was hiding behind! As he walked into the room, everyone was shocked to see his muddy and oily clothes.

The Fat Controller smiled at Lady Hatt. He knew he was dirty and a little late, but he had done his very best to get there on time, so he had kept his promise to her. "Thank you, my dear!" said Lady Hatt, as The Fat Controller gave her the lovely bunch of flowers.

She looked in surprise at his muddy
and oily jacket and his torn and
stained trousers.
"I know this is my party," she said with
a smile, "but I didn't realise it was a
fancy dress party!"

Everyone, including The Fat Controller,
laughed loudly and Lady Hatt's birthday
party began.

Gordon and the Competition

Based on *The Railway Series*
by the Rev. W. Awdry

The engines on the Island of Sodor were very excited. There was going to be a May Day celebration with music, dancing and lots of fun.

"I'm really looking forward to May Day," said Toby to his Driver as they steamed past the Scottish Castle.

Knapford station was being decorated
and The Fat Controller said the
engines could be decorated, too!

"I'm going to wear blue bunting,"
said Murdoch.
"I'm going to wear a big red banner,"
said Thomas.

"I won't wear any decorations!"
said Gordon. "Decorations are far too
undignified for an important engine
like me!"

"In that case, we'll have all the fun
without you," James said.

Thomas was bringing the maypole to
the village. As he went over the level
crossing, a farmer and his children
waved at him.

"Toot! Toot!" said Thomas in reply.

The next morning, Percy's Driver wrapped streamers and flags around his funnel. Thomas' Driver attached a red banner to Thomas. Both engines were very happy to be decorated.

They could hardly wait for the May
Day celebrations.

"We could have a prize for the Best
Dressed Engine," said James.
"It could be a competition."

"What's this? I'm sure to win any competition!" said Gordon.
"You would have to be decorated," said James.
"Not me!" said Gordon. "You'd never catch me looking so ridiculous!"

When May Day arrived, it was a
beautiful sunny day. All the engines
looked splendid, except Gordon. He
still refused to wear any decorations
at all.

Gordon told himself he was glad he wasn't taking part in the silly competition. He was much too important for that. He set off and tried to forget all about it. But secretly, Gordon felt a little left out. He wished he had joined in the fun, after all.

A colourful banner had been strung across the river bridge. It was flapping furiously in the wind. As Gordon steamed over the bridge, one end of the banner came loose. It wrapped around Gordon's firebox and flapped against his funnel.

Poor Gordon couldn't see anything!

As Gordon chugged past a station,
all the people laughed at him. Gordon
tried to whoosh the banner off, but it
wouldn't budge.

"I can't see!" Gordon whistled to his
Driver. "Stop!"
"You can't stop, Gordon," said his
Driver. "You're the Express!"
Gordon tried to go faster to shake off
the banner, but it was stuck fast.

When Gordon arrived at Knapford, the bright banner was still flapping around his funnel.

"We didn't think you wanted to be decorated," said Thomas in surprise.

"I didn't!" said Gordon.

"Your banner is very nice, Gordon,"
said Percy.

"I think Gordon has won the prize," said James. "He's definitely the Best Dressed Engine!"

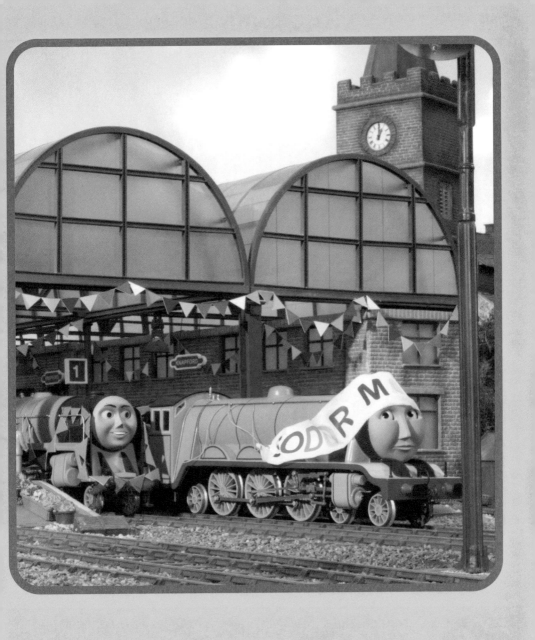

All the engines cheered and whistled.
And Gordon was secretly pleased – he
had won the competition after all!

Thomas and Percy to the Rescue

Based on *The Railway Series*
by the Rev. W. Awdry

The engines were talking in the engine shed.

"Everyone seems much happier in the springtime," said Thomas.

"But we have to work extra hard in the springtime," grumbled James. "The Fat Controller makes us travel down to the coast to work!"

"I like the salty coast air in my smokebox!" said Percy.

"Pah! It's the countryside that gets me really fired up!" snorted James, as he puffed away to collect some fuel trucks from the docks.

The Fat Controller told Thomas and Percy they would be working at the scrapyard.
"Where do you like working best?"
Percy asked Thomas, as they arrived at the scrapyard.
"I don't really mind where I work," said Thomas, "so long as I can be a Really Useful Engine."
"We'll be working hard today," said Percy.
"The Fat Controller said there is a large pile of scrap metal for us to move."

When Thomas and Percy shunted some
trucks into a siding at the scrapyard,
they saw an old coach there, looking
rather sad.

"What are you doing here?" asked Percy,
in surprise.

"They call me Old Slow Coach," she said.

"They say I'm not useful any more, so I
was sent to the scrapyard," she added,
sadly.

"You are a little dusty, but you look in
perfect shape to me," said Thomas, kindly.

"Excuse me," Percy's Driver said to the Yard Manager. "What will happen to this coach?"

"Old Slow Coach has been here for years," said the Yard Manager. "She's not useful any more, so she'll be broken up for scrap some time soon."

Thomas and Percy felt very sorry for the coach.
"We'll try and help you," said Thomas, but he really didn't know what they could do.

James whistled happily as he pulled the fuel trucks through the countryside. He was making good time, so he knew The Fat Controller would be pleased with him.

But James did not notice that one of the trucks was leaking fuel on to the track. Suddenly, a spark flew out of James' funnel and set the leaking fuel on fire!

"HELP!" whistled James in shock, as he sped along the track with clouds of smoke and flames flying out behind him.

James moved quickly off the main track
and stopped in a siding. His Driver leapt
down from the cab and rushed to the
emergency phone to call for help.

"Hello, please send help quickly," he said. "James' trucks are on fire and they're carrying fuel, so it's very dangerous!"

The Firemen set out straight away. James waited anxiously while his Driver tried to put out the fire.

Thomas and Percy had finished working
at the scrapyard. When they reached the
junction, they were surprised to see
smoke. A Guard was waving a red
warning flag at them.

"Sparks from James' funnel have caused a fire in some fuel trucks," he told them. "It's a bit of a mess, but the Firemen have now got the fire under control."

"You said the countryside got you all fired up," Percy told James, "but I didn't think you meant it this way!"

"Pah!" snorted James. "It was the stupid trucks' fault, not mine!"

"It is safe for you to move past James now!" said the Fireman to Thomas and Percy.

The engines puffed slowly past James.
They felt rather sorry for him now.

Thomas and Percy went to Tidmouth
Hault Station. The Drivers talked to the
Station Master and the engines had a
long, cool drink at the water tower.

When they had filled up their tanks,
they waited for their Drivers to return.
Suddenly, their Drivers came running
towards them.
"Are we late for something?" asked Thomas.
"We've just heard the workmen's hut at
the seaside is on fire!" said Thomas' Driver.
"Let's go and see what we can do to help."

When Thomas and Percy arrived at
the burning building, they saw the fire
engines had already arrived. The Firemen
were using hoses to fight the fire.
But they had a problem, they were about
to run out of water!

"We can't use seawater," said a Fireman, "because it clogs up our works. And if we can't find more water from somewhere, then I'm afraid we'll just have to let the workmen's hut burn!"

Thomas had a good idea. "Why don't you use the water in our tanks?" he said. "We've just refilled them at Tidmouth Hault Station, so there should be plenty for you to use!"

"You're a very clever engine!" said the Chief Fireman. He called over all the Firemen and told them about Thomas' plan. The Firemen were impressed. They quickly brought their hoses to Thomas and Percy and used the water in their tanks to tackle the fire.

Thomas and Percy watched the Firemen fight the fire. They had to use nearly all the water from the engines' tanks.

Unfortunately, when the smoke cleared, everyone could see the workmen's hut had been destroyed.

"Thank you all for your hard work," said the Foreman. "It's a terrible shame that the hut has burnt down. My workmen lived there and I don't know where they can stay now. Does anyone have any ideas?"

"I think I know where they can stay!" said Percy. "We can bring Old Slow Coach here for them to live in. She would be the perfect new home for the workmen!"

"She'll be really comfortable, too!" added Thomas.

"What a great idea, Percy!" said his Driver.

"I'll check The Fat Controller is happy for us to bring Old Slow Coach here," said Thomas' Driver.

The Fat Controller thought it was a very good idea. "I'll get the Scrapyard Manager to clean her up, so she'll be ready for you to collect her!" he said.

Old Slow Coach was now a very happy Coach indeed.

"I can't thank you enough, I feel really splendid!" she said to Thomas and Percy, as they took her down to her new home at the seaside.

When they arrived, everyone agreed there really was nothing 'Old' or 'Slow' about Coach, who would continue to be a Really Useful Coach for ever more!

The End